Weekend in Orbit

For Elisha, Esther and Miriam

First published in 2006 by Orchard Books
First paperback publication in 2007

ORCHARD BOOKS
338 Euston Road, London NW1 3BH
Orchard Books Australia
Hachette Children's Books
Level 17/207 Kent St, Sydney, NSW 2000

ISBN 1 84616 036 7 (hardback)
ISBN 1 84616 391 9 (paperback)

A CIP catalogue record for this book is available from the British Library.

1 3 5 7 9 10 8 6 4 2 (hardback)
1 3 5 7 9 10 8 6 4 2 (paperback)

Printed in Great Britain

Orchard Books is a division of Hachette Children's Books

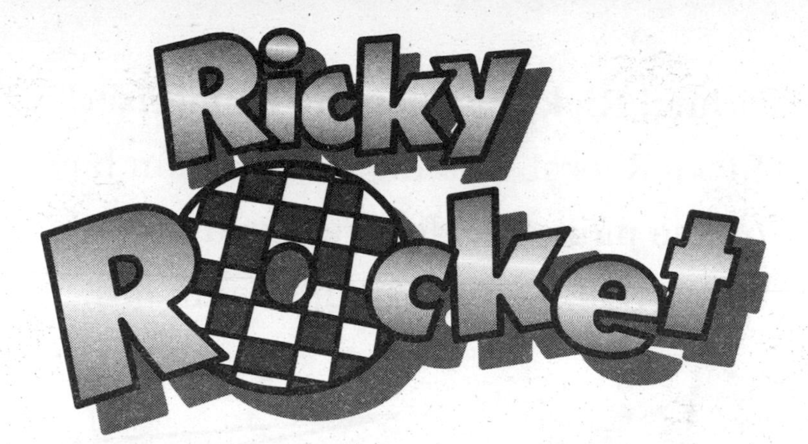

Weekend in Orbit

Shoo Rayner

ORCHARD BOOKS

"Mum! Ricky's stolen my memoriser!"

Ricky Rocket was the only human boy on the planet of Hammerhead and his sister, Sue, was the only human girl.

"Mum! Tell Ricky to give it back!" she screamed, in the ear-splitting, blood-curdling, brain-jamming way that little Earth girls are famous for all over the universe.

"Oh Mum," Ricky groaned. "I only want to borrow it. Mine's not working and I need a memoriser for weekend camp."

"Oh Ricky!" Mum grumbled. "Why didn't you say? We could have had yours mended."

Mum had to promise Sue a shopping trip so that she would let Ricky use her memoriser at weekend camp.

"Nah!" Sue trilled, triumphantly. "Shopping's much better than stupid weekend camp!"

Dad's eyes glazed over. "Ah! Weekend camp!" he sighed. "That brings back wonderful memories. You're going to have a great time getting to know your classmates better."

"Oh no!" Ricky's heart sank. "I don't want to get to know *him* better!"

Grip was climbing aboard the space bus. Grip was the biggest, meanest, ugliest creature in the class. Grip's idea of fun was to spoil things for everyone else.

"Have a lovely time, dear," said Mum, thrusting a huge bag of Space Munchies into Ricky's arms. "Just in case they don't feed you properly."

Ricky avoided Mum's sloppy kiss, and boarded the space bus.

Ricky's best friend Bubbles waved madly from the back. "Hey, Ricky! I've saved you a seat!"

Mizz Fizz zipped up and down the aisle. "Come along! Do your seatbelts up, then we can be on our way."

The door hissed shut. The engines rumbled. The bus lifted into the air and they were on their way to Camp Orbit.

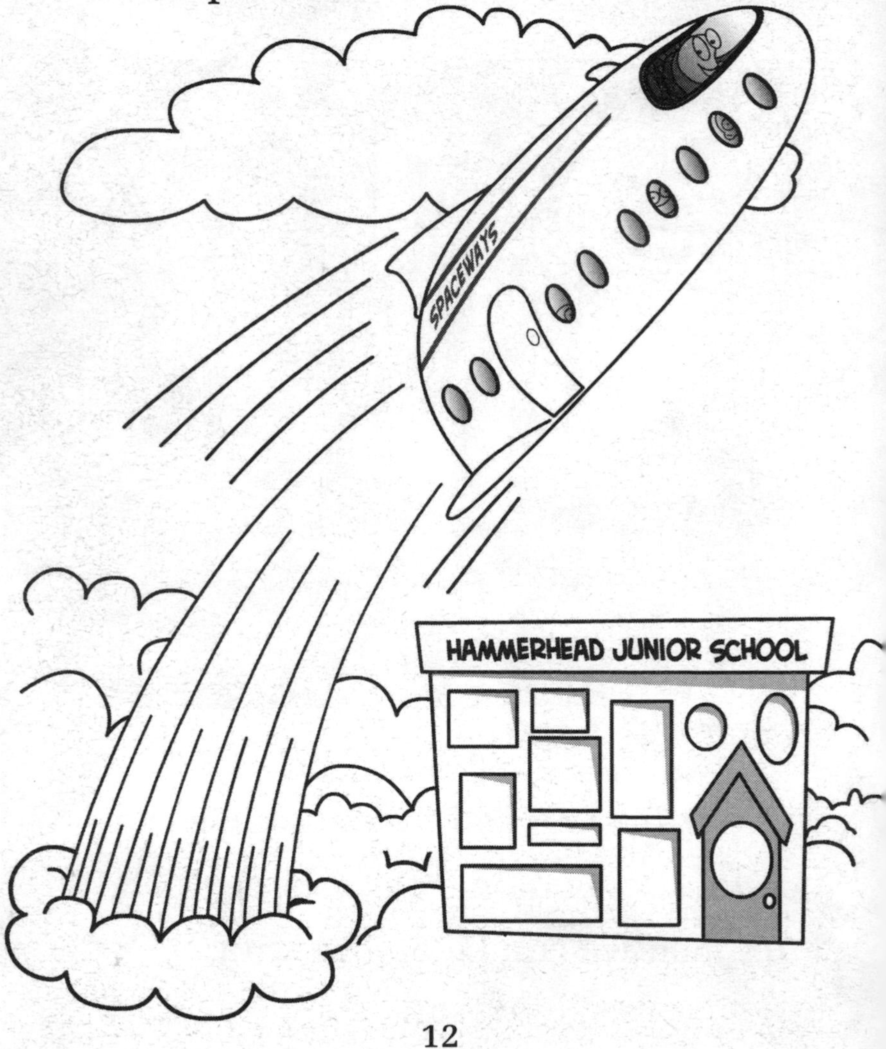

CAMP ORBIT

Camp Orbit looks like a doughnut – that's because it used to be a doughnut factory.

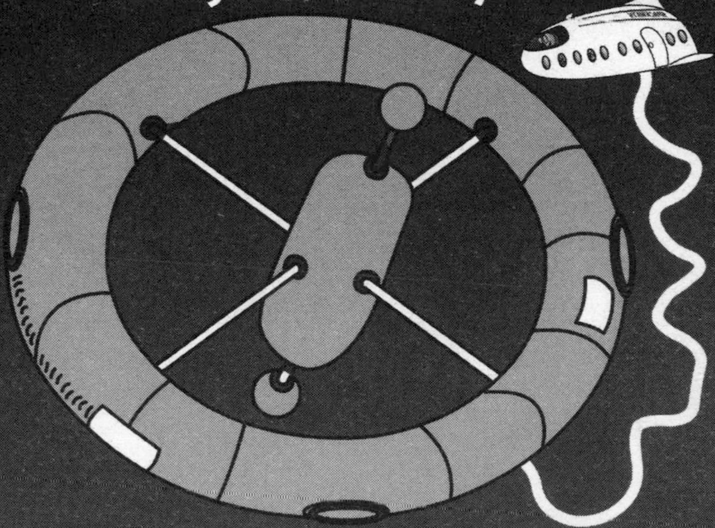

Only in the weightlessness of space could the Crepan Donut Corporation make the universally famous Lite Bite Donut[SR]

The space factory has been converted into a fun centre for school expeditions.

Safety first – in space no one can hear you scream!

Mizz Fizz checked her clipboard. "Find your dormitories and settle in first," she ordered. "Meet up for space science in one hour."

There were four corridors for the different types of creature in the class: nesters, sleepers, nappers and wide-awakes.

The bathrooms and toilets were separated for washers, lickers, groomers and *the rest*!

Ricky and Bubbles were both sleepers, so they could share a room.

RESTING AND WASHING

Resting is the polite term for "going to the toilet" in space.

When you don't know which way is up or down, it is best to go to the toilet using **tubes** or **vacuum bowls.**

SLURP! SLURP!

Washing is easy if you are a licker, but it is much harder to cough up fur balls in space.

Soap is **banned** in space – bubbles get everywhere and cause a lot of damage.

At the start of space science, Tammy Tweetle was in tears. Grip had barged into her room and found her talking to a Weeby Doll.

"Tammy hasn't got any friends to talk to," he sneered. "Tammy's best friend is a Weeby Doll!"

"In space," Mizz Fizz began, "we can do exciting experiments under weightless conditions. This morning, we shall see if weightlessness changes the way spiders weave their webs."

Everyone crowded round a glass tank containing some twigs and a large spider. The poor spider floated aimlessly, weaving a web that looked like a bowl of spaghetti.

"Over here," Mizz Fizz explained, "we have a gravity machine. "Who can tell me how it works?" A forest of hands shot up into the air.

While Karlah answered, Grip picked the spider out of the tank and waved it about menacingly. Karlah screamed and ran out of the room.

"Sorry, Mizz!" Grip smirked. "I didn't know that Karlah was scared of spiders.

After break, they went outside for a walk. "Some of us need magnetic boots to help us to stick to the surface of the space station," Mizz Fizz explained.

"These are radio aerials," she told them. "That's a docking bay. Mind those ladder rungs please...don't trip over them!"

Grip shoved Dooley in the back. Dooley tripped over a rung and started floating off towards the stars.

Everyone heard his voice crackle over their headsets, "Argh! Save me! I'm too young to die!"

Mizz Fizz flashed some purple lights and something zipped out of the docking bay. She pointed. "Here comes the emergency rescue robot."

The class cheered as the robot returned Dooley to the surface of the space station. Grip leaned over him and grinned, "Did you have a nice trip, Dooley? Ha! Ha! Ha!"

"Next," Mizz Fizz announced, "we'll be flying space trainers through an obstacle course."

Ricky and Bubbles cheered. This was what they'd had been waiting for – flying without gravity.

Ricky soon mastered the controls of his gravity-free craft. "It's amazing!" he whooped.

Bubble's voice burst over the radio. "Enemy at nine o'clock!"

Ricky looked up. Grip's ship was bearing down on him! Ricky struggled to avoid a collision. Grip barged Ricky's ship off course.

"I'll get you, Grip!" Ricky yelled, as his space trainer dived nose-first into a garbage tank.

Mizz Fizz thought they were just having a bit of fun. "Boys!" she laughed. "You're always so competitive!"

FLYING WITHOUT GRAVITY

Is Ricky upside down in this picture?

If you answer yes, you are the other way up, so YOU may be upside down!

To move in space you have to throw things. Throwing heavy stuff makes you go further.

Throwing a tennis ball makes you go a short distance.

Throwing something large, like Grip, will make you go further and faster.

Space trainers use electron traction engines. They don't need to "throw" anything. They just work – cool!

Later that day, the class went skating on the lice rink.

Grip chased Ricky and Bubbles all over the slippery surface. He knocked Bubbles over, making him land heavily on his bottom.

"I'll get you, Grip!" Bubbles yelled as a trail of purple bubbles exploded from the trumpets on his head.

Grip smirked. He was big and mean and he knew that no one dared do anything to him.

THIS WAY ROUND→
SPACE LICE
Space lice are tiny creatures that live on particles of solar wind.
If they are well fed, they will multiply until there are billions of them covering the floor of a lice rink.
The furry feelers on their heads never stop twitching. Skaters do not slide, they are carried across the rink on millions of twitching feelers.

Ricky and Bubbles made a secret pact with Tammy and Dooley to meet for a midnight feast that night.

When the alarm on Sue's memoriser bleeped, Ricky switched it off and rolled over.

"Come on, sleepyhead!" Bubbles hissed, as he dragged Ricky out of the warm, cosy bed.

They sneaked down the corridor to the common room.

"There's no one here," Bubbles whispered.

"Let's go and wake them up!" Ricky suggested.

The first room they entered glowed with a strange, green light. Something that looked like a giant insect cocoon hung from the ceiling. Ricky crept closer.

It was Grip!

The big bully was snuggled up in the cocoon like a baby. He was hugging and stroking a cuddly Sharky Nipkins, and talking to it in his sleep!

"You'll be my friend, won't you, Sharky?" Grip drooled in his sleep.

Ricky and Bubbles felt they would die trying not to laugh.

"Quick!" Ricky whispered. "Let's get the memoriser and make a video of Grip!"

SHARKY NIPKINS

Sharky Nipkins®
is a **teevee** program
for Hammerhead toddlers.

Sharky looks **fierce** to humans but
he's **cute** and cuddly to Hammerheads.
The toys are made with **cuddly**
sandpaper skin, **laser** eyes and
razor sharp teeth.

Here are some
of Sharky's
teevee pals:

Heptopuss

Sneel

Grab

The next day, Grip pushed his way to the front of the breakfast queue. He piled his tray full of food and sat down at an empty table.

Ricky and Bubbles sat down opposite him.

“Ooh, Grip!” Bubbles giggled. ”That’s a lot of Saturn Toasties you’ve got there.”

“Are you going to save some for your little friend Sharky Nipkins?” Ricky chuckled and showed Grip the screen of the memoriser.

Grip hurled his chair back and leaned across the table. His eyes glowed red as he stared hard at Ricky.

Ricky's stomach lurched. Had he pushed Grip too far? Grip looked as if he would eat *him* for breakfast!

Then...slowly...Grip looked away, picked up his chair, sat down and finished his breakfast in silence.

The rest of the weekend was amazing.

"This has been the best time ever!" Ricky told Bubbles as they jumped about on the Rampoline.

“Yeah!” Bubbles laughed, popping out some multicoloured bubbles. “No more trouble from Grip. Not in Tec Design or Freefall…not even at the Lunar Disco last night!”

“He knew we’d tell everyone about his Sharky Nipkins otherwise!” Ricky grinned.

"Where's my memoriser?" Sue whined as soon as Ricky was home again. "You'd better not have broken it!"

"Of course not," said Ricky. "I took very special care of it. I got some unbelievable video on it!"

"I told you you'd have a good time," Dad said smugly. "Did you get to know your classmates better, like I said?"

Ricky grinned. "Oh yes, Dad! I got to know them *really* well!"

Ricky Rocket

Shoo Rayner

Enjoy all these Ricky Rocket stories!

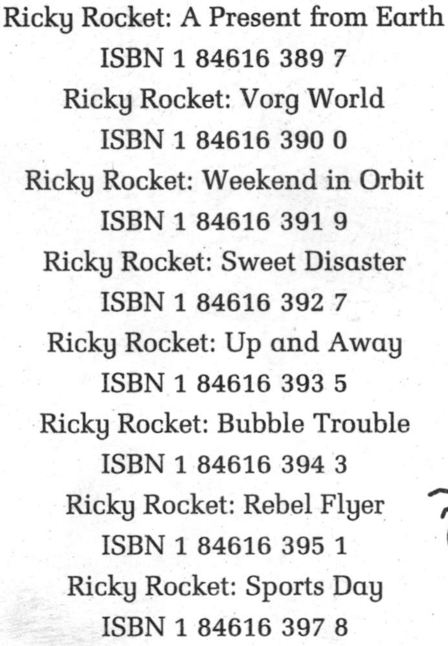

Ricky Rocket: A Present from Earth

ISBN 1 84616 389 7

Ricky Rocket: Vorg World

ISBN 1 84616 390 0

Ricky Rocket: Weekend in Orbit

ISBN 1 84616 391 9

Ricky Rocket: Sweet Disaster

ISBN 1 84616 392 7

Ricky Rocket: Up and Away

ISBN 1 84616 393 5

Ricky Rocket: Bubble Trouble

ISBN 1 84616 394 3

Ricky Rocket: Rebel Flyer

ISBN 1 84616 395 1

Ricky Rocket: Sports Day

ISBN 1 84616 397 8

All priced at £3.99

Orchard Crunchies are available from all good bookshops, or can be ordered direct from the publisher: Orchard Books, PO BOX 29, Douglas IM99 1BQ
Credit card orders please telephone 01624 836000 or fax 01624 837033
or visit our internet site: www.wattspub.co.uk or e-mail: bookshop@enterprise.net for details.

To order please quote title, author and ISBN and your full name and address.
Cheques and postal orders should be made payable to 'Bookpost plc.'
Postage and packing is FREE within the UK
(overseas customers should add £1.00 per book).

Prices and availability are subject to change.